ACCELERATED READER

LEVEL _5.1_

POINTS _1_

QUIZ _179838_

SiLLy StoRieS

The Blind Men and the Elephant

and Other Silly Stories

Compiled by Vic Parker

Gareth Stevens
PUBLISHING

Please visit our website, **www.garethstevens.com**.
For a free color catalog of all our high-quality books,
call toll free 1-800-542-2595 or fax 1-877-542-2596.

Cataloging-in-Publication Data
Parker, Vic.
The blind men and the elephant and other silly stories / by Vic Parker.
p. cm. — (Silly stories)
Includes index.
ISBN 978-1-4824-4195-6 (pbk.)
ISBN 978-1-4824-4196-3 (6 pack)
ISBN 978-1-4824-4197-0 (library binding)
1. Children's stories. 2. Folklore. 3. Humorous stories.
I. Parker, Victoria. II. Title.
PZ8.P35 Bl 2016
398.2—d23

Published in 2016 by
Gareth Stevens Publishing
111 East 14th Street, Suite 349
New York, NY 10003

Copyright © 2016 Miles Kelly Publishing

Publishing Director | Belinda Gallagher
Creative Director | Jo Cowan
Editorial Director | Rosie McGuire
Senior Editor | Carly Blake
Editorial Assistant | Amy Johnson
Designer | Joe Jones
Production Manager | Elizabeth Collins
Reprographics | Stephan Davis, Jennifer Hunt, Thom Allaway

Acknowlegments:
The publishers would like to thank the following artists who have
contributed to this book:
Beehive Illustration Agency: Rosie Brooks, Mike Phillips (inc. cover)
Jan Lewis, Aimee Mappley (decorative frames)
All other artwork from the Miles Kelly Artwork Bank

Printed in the United States of America

CPSIA compliance information: Batch # CW16GS:
For further information contact Gareth Stevens, New York, New York at 1-800-542-2595.

Contents

The Simpleton

By Andrew Lang

Once upon a time there lived a man
who was as rich as he could be, but as no
happiness in this world is ever quite
complete, he had an only son who was such
a simpleton that he could barely add two
and two together. At last his father
determined to put up with his stupidity no
longer and, giving him a purse full of gold,
sent him to seek his fortune in foreign lands,

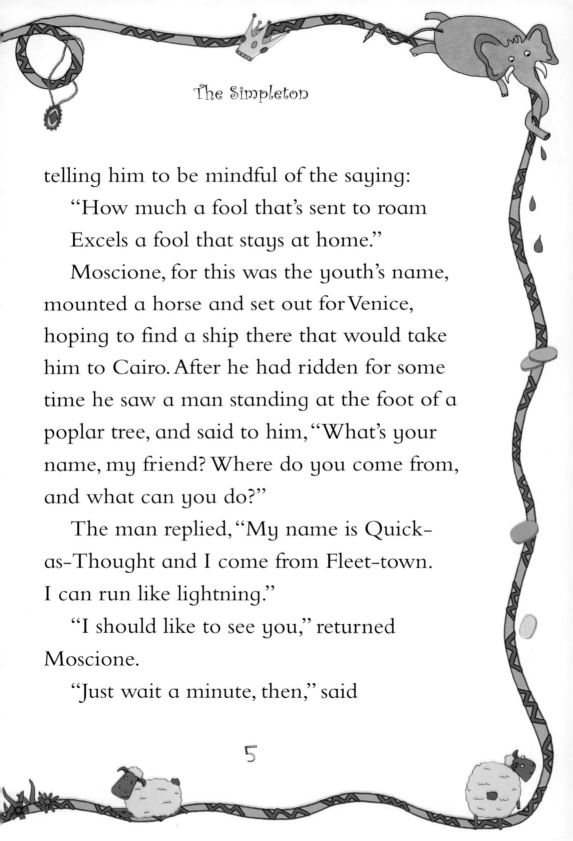

telling him to be mindful of the saying:

"How much a fool that's sent to roam

Excels a fool that stays at home."

Moscione, for this was the youth's name, mounted a horse and set out for Venice, hoping to find a ship there that would take him to Cairo. After he had ridden for some time he saw a man standing at the foot of a poplar tree, and said to him, "What's your name, my friend? Where do you come from, and what can you do?"

The man replied, "My name is Quick-as-Thought and I come from Fleet-town. I can run like lightning."

"I should like to see you," returned Moscione.

"Just wait a minute, then," said

The Simpleton

Quick-as-Thought, "and I will soon show you that I am speaking the truth."

The words were hardly out of his mouth when a young doe ran right across the field they were standing in.

Quick-as-Thought let her run a short distance, in order to give her a start, and then pursued her so quickly and so lightly that you could not have tracked his footsteps if the field had been strewn with flour. In a few springs he had overtaken the doe.

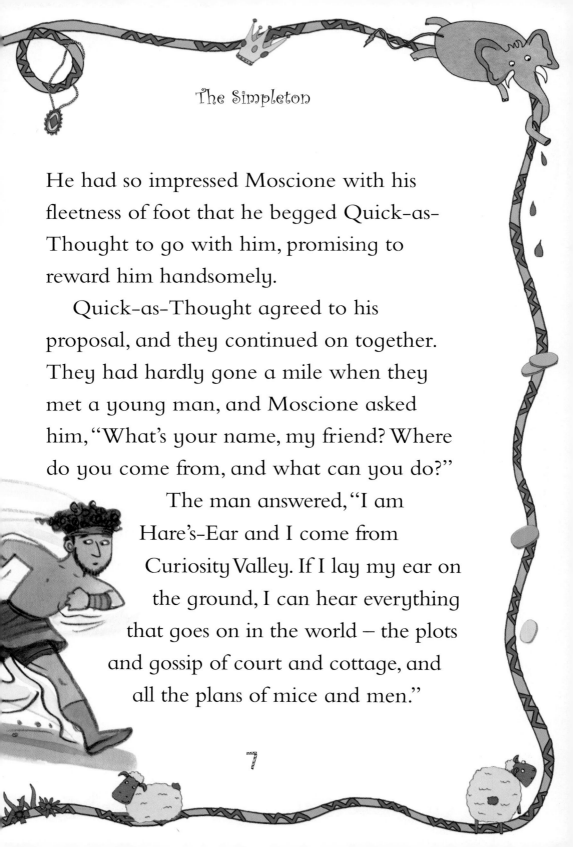

The Simpleton

He had so impressed Moscione with his fleetness of foot that he begged Quick-as-Thought to go with him, promising to reward him handsomely.

Quick-as-Thought agreed to his proposal, and they continued on together. They had hardly gone a mile when they met a young man, and Moscione asked him, "What's your name, my friend? Where do you come from, and what can you do?"

The man answered, "I am Hare's-Ear and I come from Curiosity Valley. If I lay my ear on the ground, I can hear everything that goes on in the world – the plots and gossip of court and cottage, and all the plans of mice and men."

"If that's the case," replied Moscione, "tell me what's going on in my home at present."

The youth laid his ear to the ground and at once reported, "An old man is saying to his wife, 'Heaven be praised that we have got rid of Moscione, for perhaps, when he has been out in the world a little, he may gain some common sense, and return home less of a fool than when he set out.'"

"Enough, enough," cried Moscione. "You speak the truth, and I believe you. Come with us and your fortune's made."

The young man consented, and after they had gone about ten miles, they met a third man, to whom Moscione said, "What's your name, my brave fellow? Where were you born, and what can you do?"

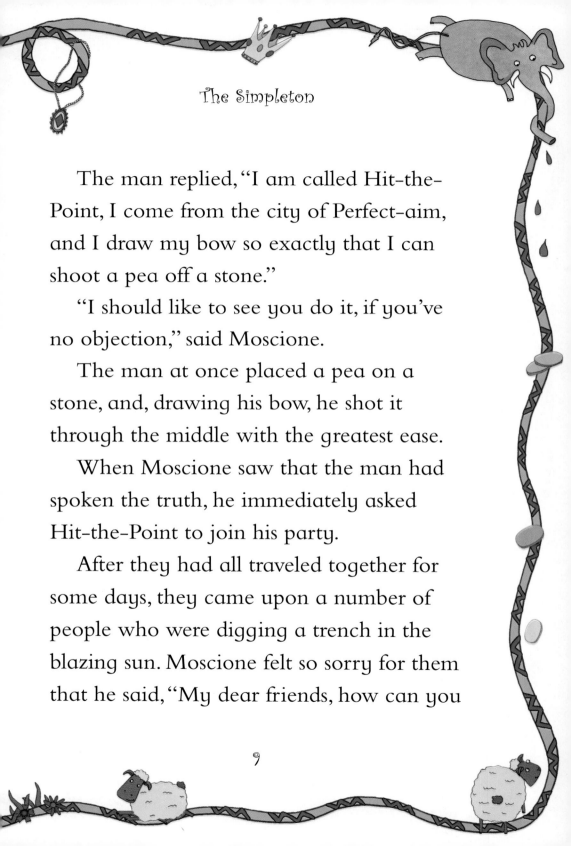

The Simpleton

The man replied, "I am called Hit-the-Point, I come from the city of Perfect-aim, and I draw my bow so exactly that I can shoot a pea off a stone."

"I should like to see you do it, if you've no objection," said Moscione.

The man at once placed a pea on a stone, and, drawing his bow, he shot it through the middle with the greatest ease.

When Moscione saw that the man had spoken the truth, he immediately asked Hit-the-Point to join his party.

After they had all traveled together for some days, they came upon a number of people who were digging a trench in the blazing sun. Moscione felt so sorry for them that he said, "My dear friends, how can you

9

stand working so hard in heat that would cook an egg in a minute?"

But one of the workmen answered, "We are as fresh as daisies, for we have a young man among us who blows on our backs like the west wind."

The youth was called, and Moscione asked him, "What's your name? Where do you come from, and what can you do?"

He answered, "I am called Blow-Blast. I come from Wind-town, and with my mouth I can make any winds you please. If you wish a west wind I can raise it for you in a second, but if you prefer a north wind I can blow these houses down before your eyes."

"Seeing is believing," returned Moscione. Blow-Blast at once began to convince

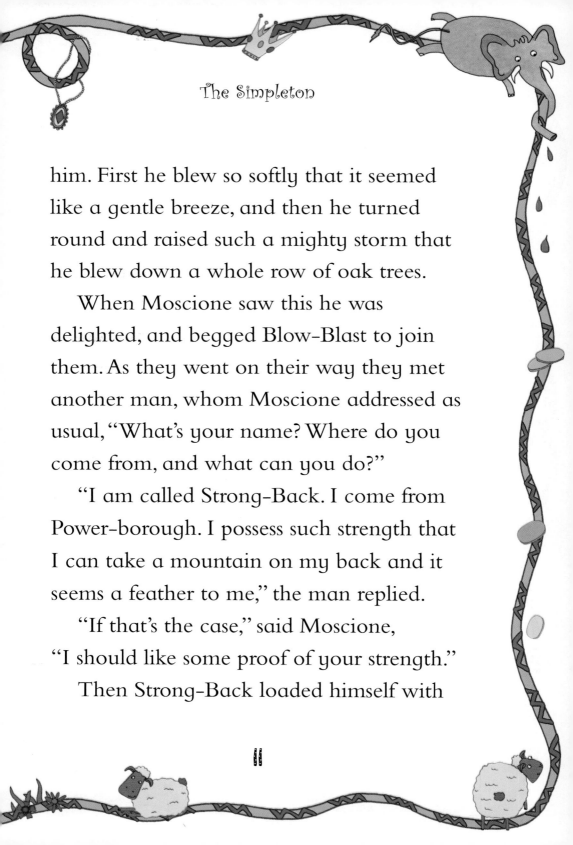

him. First he blew so softly that it seemed like a gentle breeze, and then he turned round and raised such a mighty storm that he blew down a whole row of oak trees.

When Moscione saw this he was delighted, and begged Blow-Blast to join them. As they went on their way they met another man, whom Moscione addressed as usual, "What's your name? Where do you come from, and what can you do?"

"I am called Strong-Back. I come from Power-borough. I possess such strength that I can take a mountain on my back and it seems a feather to me," the man replied.

"If that's the case," said Moscione, "I should like some proof of your strength."

Then Strong-Back loaded himself with

11

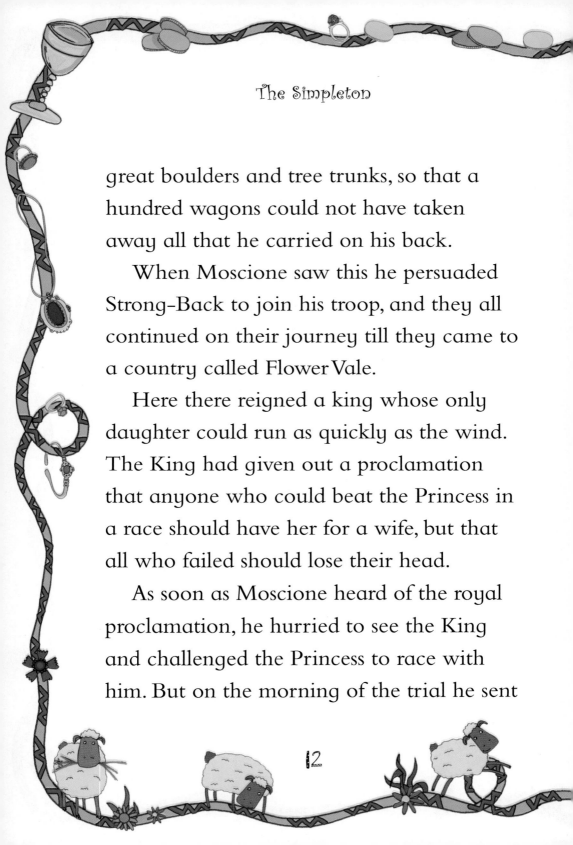

great boulders and tree trunks, so that a hundred wagons could not have taken away all that he carried on his back.

When Moscione saw this he persuaded Strong-Back to join his troop, and they all continued on their journey till they came to a country called Flower Vale.

Here there reigned a king whose only daughter could run as quickly as the wind. The King had given out a proclamation that anyone who could beat the Princess in a race should have her for a wife, but that all who failed should lose their head.

As soon as Moscione heard of the royal proclamation, he hurried to see the King and challenged the Princess to race with him. But on the morning of the trial he sent

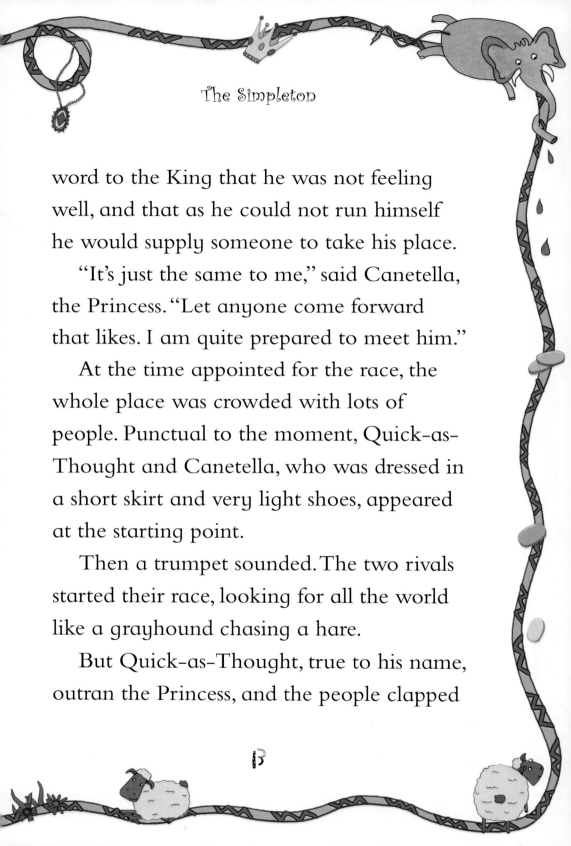

word to the King that he was not feeling
well, and that as he could not run himself
he would supply someone to take his place.

"It's just the same to me," said Canetella,
the Princess. "Let anyone come forward
that likes. I am quite prepared to meet him."

At the time appointed for the race, the
whole place was crowded with lots of
people. Punctual to the moment, Quick-as-
Thought and Canetella, who was dressed in
a short skirt and very light shoes, appeared
at the starting point.

Then a trumpet sounded. The two rivals
started their race, looking for all the world
like a grayhound chasing a hare.

But Quick-as-Thought, true to his name,
outran the Princess, and the people clapped

and shouted, "Long live the stranger!"

Canetella was very fed up at being beaten, but, as the race had to be run a second time, she determined she would not be beaten again. She went home and sent Quick-as-Thought a magic ring. It prevented the wearer not only from running, but even from walking. The Princess begged him to wear it for her sake.

Next morning the crowd assembled, and Canetella and Quick-as-Thought began their trial afresh. The Princess ran as quickly as ever, but Quick-as-Thought was like an overloaded donkey, and could not go a step.

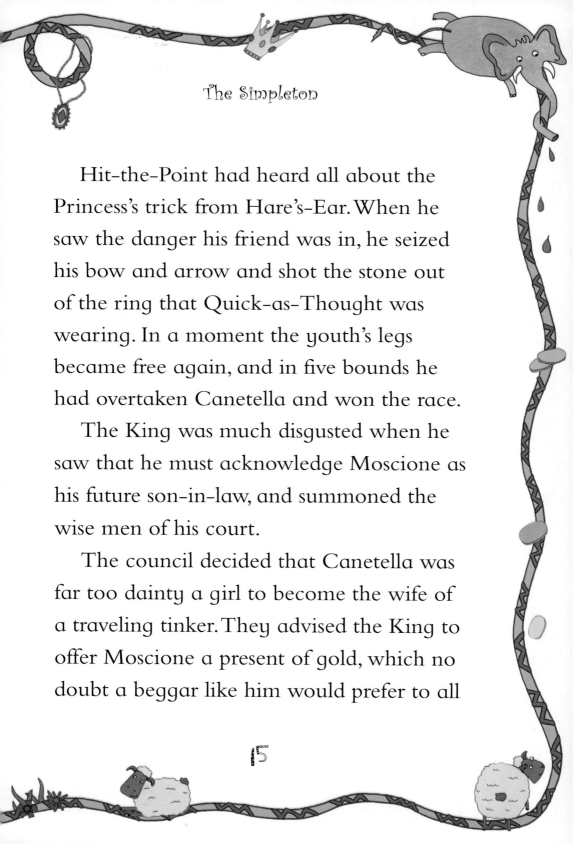

The Simpleton

Hit-the-Point had heard all about the Princess's trick from Hare's-Ear. When he saw the danger his friend was in, he seized his bow and arrow and shot the stone out of the ring that Quick-as-Thought was wearing. In a moment the youth's legs became free again, and in five bounds he had overtaken Canetella and won the race.

The King was much disgusted when he saw that he must acknowledge Moscione as his future son-in-law, and summoned the wise men of his court.

The council decided that Canetella was far too dainty a girl to become the wife of a traveling tinker. They advised the King to offer Moscione a present of gold, which no doubt a beggar like him would prefer to all

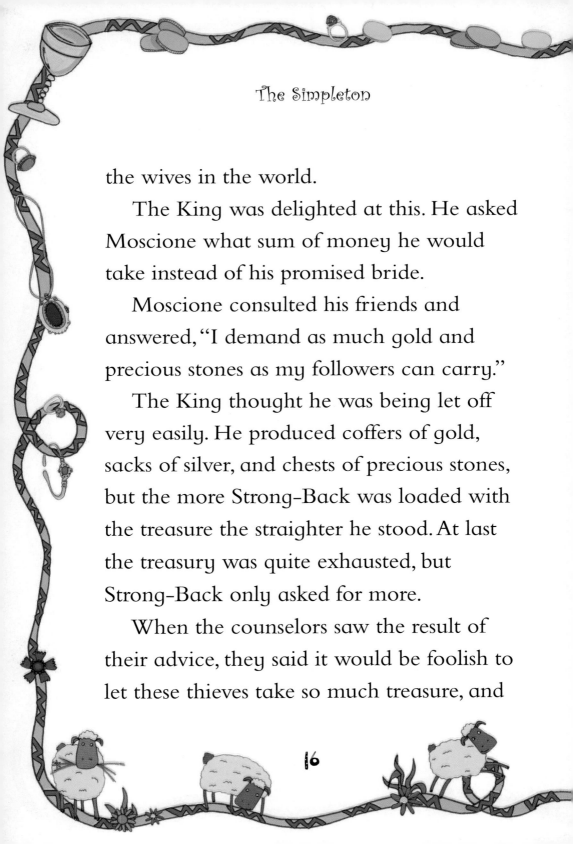

the wives in the world.

The King was delighted at this. He asked Moscione what sum of money he would take instead of his promised bride.

Moscione consulted his friends and answered, "I demand as much gold and precious stones as my followers can carry."

The King thought he was being let off very easily. He produced coffers of gold, sacks of silver, and chests of precious stones, but the more Strong-Back was loaded with the treasure the straighter he stood. At last the treasury was quite exhausted, but Strong-Back only asked for more.

When the counselors saw the result of their advice, they said it would be foolish to let these thieves take so much treasure, and

17

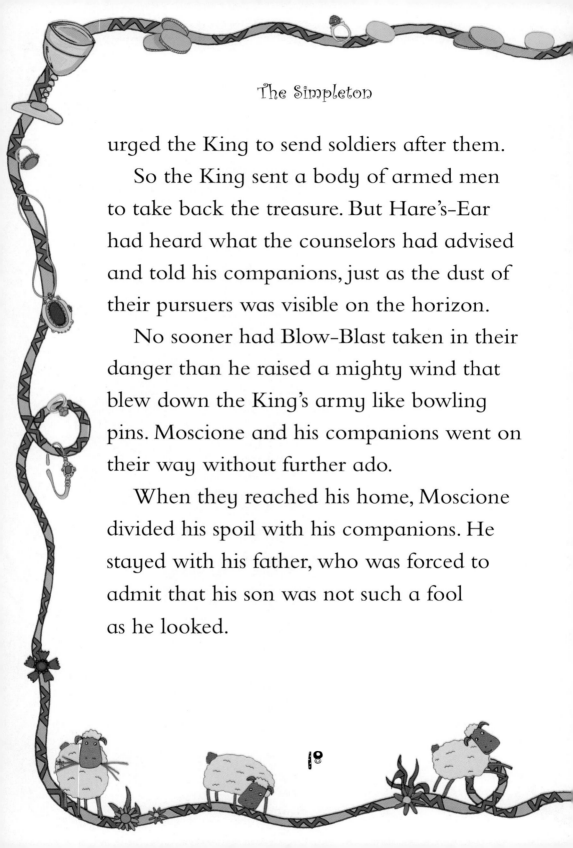

urged the King to send soldiers after them.

So the King sent a body of armed men to take back the treasure. But Hare's-Ear had heard what the counselors had advised and told his companions, just as the dust of their pursuers was visible on the horizon.

No sooner had Blow-Blast taken in their danger than he raised a mighty wind that blew down the King's army like bowling pins. Moscione and his companions went on their way without further ado.

When they reached his home, Moscione divided his spoil with his companions. He stayed with his father, who was forced to admit that his son was not such a fool as he looked.

The Foolish Weaver

By Andrew Lang

Once there was a weaver who was in want of work, and he took service with a farmer as a shepherd. The farmer knew that the man was very slow-witted and gave him very careful instructions as to everything that he was to do. He ended up by saying, "If a wolf or any wild animal tries to hurt the flock, you should pick up a big stone like this" – and he demonstrated – "and

19

The Foolish Weaver

throw a few at him. He will be afraid and run away." The weaver said that he understood, and set off, taking the sheep to the hills to graze.

By chance in the afternoon a leopard appeared, so the weaver instantly ran home as fast as he could to get the stones which the farmer had shown him, to throw at the creature. When he came back all the flock were scattered or killed!

When the farmer heard the tale he gave the weaver a sound scolding. "Were there no stones on

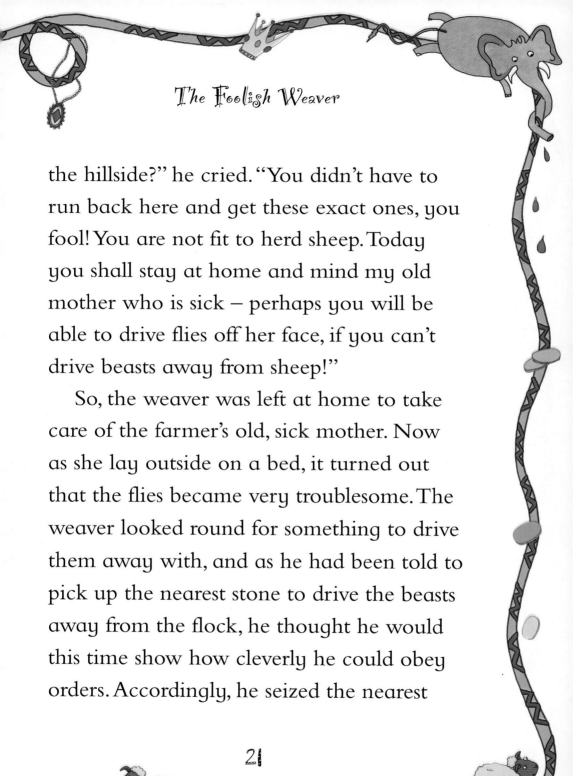

the hillside?" he cried. "You didn't have to run back here and get these exact ones, you fool! You are not fit to herd sheep. Today you shall stay at home and mind my old mother who is sick – perhaps you will be able to drive flies off her face, if you can't drive beasts away from sheep!"

So, the weaver was left at home to take care of the farmer's old, sick mother. Now as she lay outside on a bed, it turned out that the flies became very troublesome. The weaver looked round for something to drive them away with, and as he had been told to pick up the nearest stone to drive the beasts away from the flock, he thought he would this time show how cleverly he could obey orders. Accordingly, he seized the nearest

stone, which was a big, heavy one, and tossed it at the flies. Of course, very unhappily, he killed the poor old woman also! Then, being afraid of the wrath of the farmer, he fled and was not seen again in that neighborhood.

All that day and all the next night he walked, and eventually he came to a village where a great many weavers lived together.

"You are welcome," said they. "Eat and sleep, for tomorrow six of us start in search of fresh wool to weave, and we pray you to give us your company."

The Foolish Weaver

"Willingly," answered the weaver. So the next morning the seven weavers set out to go to the village where they could buy what they wanted. On the way they had to cross a ravine, which lately had been full of water, but now was quite dry. However, the weavers were accustomed to swimming over this ravine. Regardless of the fact that it was dry, they stripped and, tying their clothes on their heads, started to swim across the dry sand and rocks that formed the bed of the ravine. The weavers got to the other side without further damage than bruised knees and elbows, and as soon as they were over, one of them began to count everybody to make sure that all were safely there. He counted all except himself, and then cried out that somebody was missing! This set each of them counting, but each made the same mistake of counting all except himself, so that they became certain that one of them was missing! They ran up and down the bank of the ravine, wringing their hands in great distress and looking for signs of their lost comrade.

Then a farmer found them and asked what was the matter. "Alas!" said one. "Seven of us started from the other bank and one must have been drowned on the

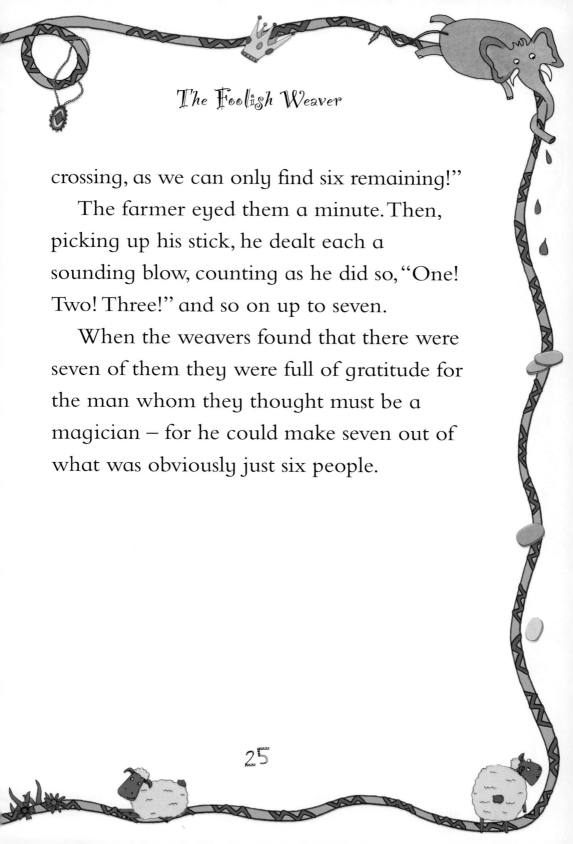

crossing, as we can only find six remaining!"

The farmer eyed them a minute. Then, picking up his stick, he dealt each a sounding blow, counting as he did so, "One! Two! Three!" and so on up to seven.

When the weavers found that there were seven of them they were full of gratitude for the man whom they thought must be a magician – for he could make seven out of what was obviously just six people.

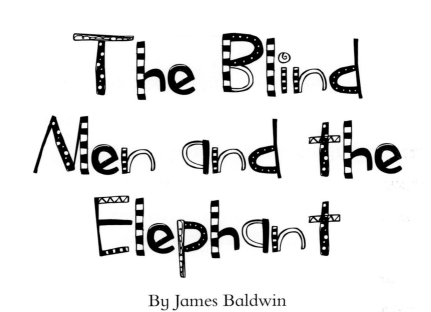

The Blind Men and the Elephant

By James Baldwin

There were once six blind men who stood by the roadside every day, and scraped out a living by begging from the people who passed. They knew that all sorts of sights passed them by, for they heard all the talk of the travelers who went up and down the road. But they had never seen anything, for being blind, how could they?

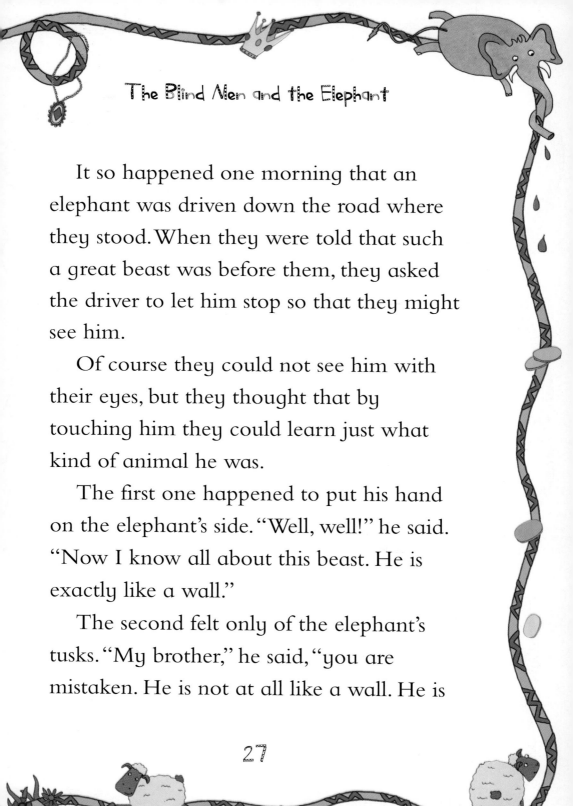

The Blind Men and the Elephant

It so happened one morning that an elephant was driven down the road where they stood. When they were told that such a great beast was before them, they asked the driver to let him stop so that they might see him.

Of course they could not see him with their eyes, but they thought that by touching him they could learn just what kind of animal he was.

The first one happened to put his hand on the elephant's side. "Well, well!" he said. "Now I know all about this beast. He is exactly like a wall."

The second felt only of the elephant's tusks. "My brother," he said, "you are mistaken. He is not at all like a wall. He is

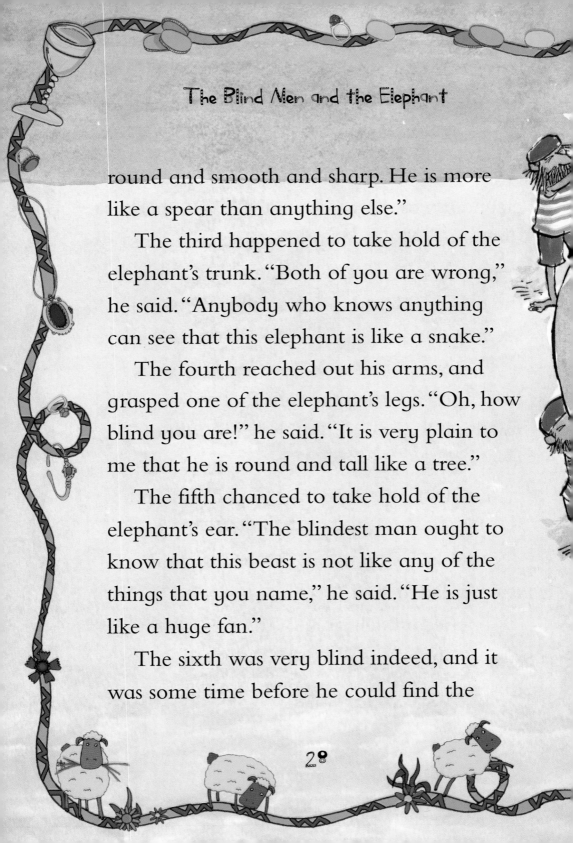

round and smooth and sharp. He is more like a spear than anything else."

The third happened to take hold of the elephant's trunk. "Both of you are wrong," he said. "Anybody who knows anything can see that this elephant is like a snake."

The fourth reached out his arms, and grasped one of the elephant's legs. "Oh, how blind you are!" he said. "It is very plain to me that he is round and tall like a tree."

The fifth chanced to take hold of the elephant's ear. "The blindest man ought to know that this beast is not like any of the things that you name," he said. "He is just like a huge fan."

The sixth was very blind indeed, and it was some time before he could find the

The Blind Men and the Elephant

elephant at all. At last he seized the animal's tail. "O foolish fellows!" he cried. "You surely have lost your senses. This elephant is not like a wall, or a spear, or a snake, or a tree, neither is he like a fan. But any man with a particle of sense can see that he is exactly like a rope."

Then the elephant moved on, and the six blind men sat by the roadside all day, and argued about it. Each believed that he knew just how the animal looked, and each called the others names because they did not agree with him.

People who have eyes sometimes act just as foolishly.

The Field of Boliauns

By Joseph Jacobs

One fine day at harvest, in holiday time, when the sun blazed high over the wheat fields, Tom Fitzpatrick was taking a ramble through the country. He went along the shady side of a field, when all of a sudden he heard a clacking sort of noise nearby.

"Dear me," said Tom, "but isn't it surprising to hear the stone-chatters singing

so late in the season?" So Tom crept ahead,
going on the tips of his toes to try to get a
sight of what was making the noise, to see
if he was right in his guess.

The noise stopped, but as Tom looked
sharply through the bushes, what
should he see in a nook of the
hedge but a brown jug, that
might hold about a gallon
and a half of liquid. Then,
a tiny bit of an old man
sauntered up, with a jaunty
little hat stuck upon the
top of his head. He pulled
out a little wooden stool
and stood up upon it,
then dipped a little mug

into the pitcher, took it out full and put it beside the stool. Then he sat down under the pitcher, and began to work at cobbling a shoe, putting a heel piece on a pointy-toed shoe just fit for himself.

"Well, by the powers," said Tom to himself, "I often heard tell of the Leprechauns, and, to tell God's truth, I never rightly believed in them — but here's one of them in real life. If I play my cards right, I can make my fortune. They say a body must never take their eyes off them, or they'll escape."

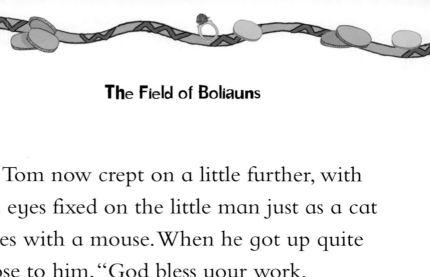

The Field of Boliauns

Tom now crept on a little further, with his eyes fixed on the little man just as a cat does with a mouse. When he got up quite close to him, "God bless your work, neighbor," said Tom.

The little man raised up his head, and, "Thank you kindly," said he.

"I wonder why you'd be working on the holiday!" said Tom.

"That's my own business, not yours," was the reply.

"Well, maybe you'd be civil enough to tell us what you've got in the jug there?" said Tom.

"That I will, with pleasure," said he. "It's good ale."

"Ale!" said Tom. "Thunder and fire!

Where did you get it?"

"Where did I get it, is it? Why, I made it. And what do you think I made it of?"

"I haven't a clue," said Tom. "Malt, I suppose, at a guess."

"Wrong!" announced the brownie gleefully. "I made it out of grass."

"Of grass!" said Tom, bursting out laughing. "Sure you don't think me to be such a fool as to believe that?"

"Do as you please," said he, "but what I tell you is the truth. Did you never hear tell of the Vikings?"

"Well, what about them?" said Tom.

"Why, when they were here they taught us to make ale out of the grass, and the secret's been in my family ever since."

The Field of Boliauns

"Will you give me a taste of your beer?" said Tom.

"I'll tell you what it is, young man, it would be fitter for you to be looking after your father's property than to be bothering decent quiet people with your foolish questions. There now, while you're idling away your time here, the cows have broken into the oats, and are knocking the wheat all about."

Tom was taken so by surprise with this that he was just on the very point of turning round... but he suddenly realized that the Leprechaun might be up to a trick. He collected himself, made a grab at the Leprechaun, and caught him up in his hand. However, in his hurry he knocked over the jug and spilled all the ale, so that

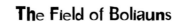

he could not get a taste of it to tell what sort it was. Tom then swore that he would kill the Leprechaun if he did not show him where his money was.

Tom looked so wicked and determined that the little man was quite frightened, so said the Leprechaun, "Come along with me a couple of fields off and I will show you a pot of gold."

So they went, and Tom held the Leprechaun tightly in his hand, and never took his eyes off him. They had to cross hedges and ditches, and a crooked bit of bog, till at last they came to a great field all full of boliaun plants. The Leprechaun pointed to a big boliaun, and says he, "Dig under that boliaun, and you'll get the great pot all full of coins."

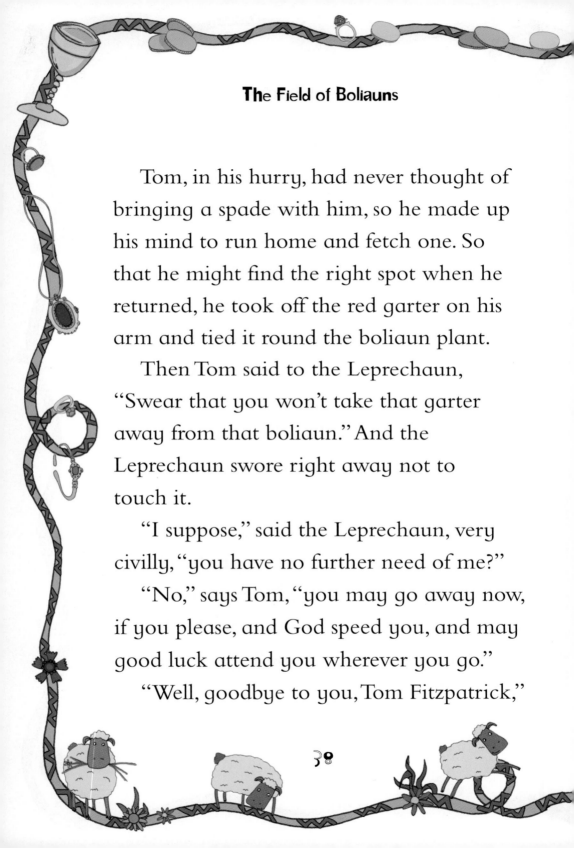

The Field of Boliauns

Tom, in his hurry, had never thought of bringing a spade with him, so he made up his mind to run home and fetch one. So that he might find the right spot when he returned, he took off the red garter on his arm and tied it round the boliaun plant.

Then Tom said to the Leprechaun, "Swear that you won't take that garter away from that boliaun." And the Leprechaun swore right away not to touch it.

"I suppose," said the Leprechaun, very civilly, "you have no further need of me?"

"No," says Tom, "you may go away now, if you please, and God speed you, and may good luck attend you wherever you go."

"Well, goodbye to you, Tom Fitzpatrick,"

said the Leprechaun, "and much good may it do you when you get it."

So Tom ran for dear life, till he came home and got a spade, and then away with him, as hard as he could go, back to the field of boliauns. But when he got there,

lo and behold! Every single boliaun in the field had a red garter tied about it!

"Whatever do I do now?" gasped Tom in exasperation. "I can't dig up the whole field, that's for sure – there's more than forty good Irish acres in it!"

So Tom came home again with his spade on his shoulder, a little cooler than he went, and many's the hearty curse he gave the Leprechaun every time he thought of the turn he had served him.